MR. GOOD

Roger Hargreaves

Written and illustrated by
Adam Hargreaves

Mr Good is very good.

He always makes his bed.
He always cleans his teeth.
And he always wipes his feet.

He never slams doors.
He never forgets birthdays.
And he never, ever tells lies.

Mr Good is very, very good.

However, Mr Good lives in a place called Badland.

A place where nobody is like Mr Good.

A place where people do slam doors.

And they slam them in your face!

In Badland, the puddles are much deeper than they look.

In Badland, a dog's bite is worse than its bark.

In Badland, even the trees are bad!

One day it was wet and windy.

Well, of course it was.

The weather is always bad in Badland.

Mr Good was walking along minding his own business when the hat of the man in front blew off.

Mr Good leapt in the air and caught it for him.

The man turned round and glared at Mr Good.

"What do you think you're doing?" he thundered. "Give my hat back!"

Poor Mr Good.

This sort of thing was always happening to him.

You see, the very idea of doing a good deed in Badland was preposterous, unthinkable, mad.

If Mr Good offered to help carry shopping, he was accused of stealing.

If he kindly held a door open for someone,
then he would be kicked in the shin!

Not surprisingly, Mr Good was not very happy.

In fact, he was miserable.

So he decided to go for a long walk to think about things.

He walked for a very long time.

He was so deep in thought that he did not notice how far he had gone.

And he was so deep in thought that he accidentally walked slap bang into somebody.

 "Oh . . . oh . . . I . . . I . . . I'm s-s-so s-s-sorry," stammered Mr Good, nervously.

"That's quite all right," said the man, and carried on his way.

"Quite all right," repeated Mr Good to himself. "That's quite all right?"

In the whole of his life no one had ever said 'that's quite all right' to Mr Good.

Then Mr Good noticed that the sun was shining.

Which was strange, because the sun never shone in Badland.

Further on, Mr Good found a dustbin on its side.

Without thinking, he tidied up all the rubbish.

"Thank you," said a woman.

Mr Good stared at her.

In the whole of his life no one had ever said 'thank you' to him.

"Could you tell me where I am?" he asked.

"You're in Goodland," replied the woman.

"Thank you," said Mr Good.

"My pleasure," said the woman.

Mr Good beamed.

And I am sure you have guessed that Mr Good now lives in Goodland.

And Mr Good is happy.

Very, very happy doing good deeds all day long.

The only thing Mr Good still does not trust are puddles.

Once you have stepped in a Badland puddle, you never forget!

3 Great Offers for MR.MEN Fans!

MR.MEN TOKEN

1 New Mr. Men or Little Miss Library Bus Presentation Cases

A brand new stronger, roomier school bus library box, with sturdy carrying handle and stay-closed fasteners.
The full colour, wipe-clean boxes make a great home for your full collection.
They're just £5.99 inc P&P and free bookmark!

☐ MR. MEN ☐ LITTLE MISS (please tick and order overleaf)

2 Door Hangers and Posters

In every Mr. Men and Little Miss book like this one, you will find a special token. Collect 6 tokens and we will send you a brilliant Mr. Men or Little Miss poster and a Mr. Men or Little Miss double sided full colour bedroom door hanger of your choice. Simply tick your choice in the list and tape a 50p coin for your two items to this page.

PLEASE STICK YOUR 50P COIN HERE

Door Hangers (please tick)
☐ Mr. Nosey & Mr. Muddle
☐ Mr. Slow & Mr. Busy
☐ Mr. Messy & Mr. Quiet
☐ Mr. Perfect & Mr. Forgetful
☐ Little Miss Fun & Little Miss Late
☐ Little Miss Helpful & Little Miss Tidy
☐ Little Miss Busy & Little Miss Brainy
☐ Little Miss Star & Little Miss Fun

Posters (please tick)
☐ MR.MEN
☐ LITTLE MISS

3 Sixteen Beautiful Fridge Magnets – any 2 for £2.00!
inc.P&P

They're very special collector's items!
Simply tick your first and second* choices from the list below
of any 2 characters!

1st Choice

- [ ] Mr. Happy
- [ ] Mr. Lazy
- [ ] Mr. Topsy-Turvy
- [ ] Mr. Bounce
- [ ] Mr. Bump
- [ ] Mr. Small
- [ ] Mr. Snow
- [ ] Mr. Wrong

- [ ] Mr. Daydream
- [ ] Mr. Tickle
- [ ] Mr. Greedy
- [ ] Mr. Funny
- [ ] Little Miss Giggles
- [ ] Little Miss Splendid
- [ ] Little Miss Naughty
- [ ] Little Miss Sunshine

2nd Choice

- [ ] Mr. Happy
- [ ] Mr. Lazy
- [ ] Mr. Topsy-Turvy
- [ ] Mr. Bounce
- [ ] Mr. Bump
- [ ] Mr. Small
- [ ] Mr. Snow
- [ ] Mr. Wrong

- [ ] Mr. Daydream
- [ ] Mr. Tickle
- [ ] Mr. Greedy
- [ ] Mr. Funny
- [ ] Little Miss Giggles
- [ ] Little Miss Splendid
- [ ] Little Miss Naughty
- [ ] Little Miss Sunshine

*Only in case your first choice is out of stock.

TO BE COMPLETED BY AN ADULT

**To apply for any of these great offers, ask an adult to complete the coupon below and send it with
the appropriate payment and tokens, if needed, to MR. MEN OFFERS, PO BOX 7, MANCHESTER M19 2HD**

- [ ] Please send _____ Mr. Men Library case(s) and/or _____ Little Miss Library case(s) at £5.99 each inc P&P
- [ ] Please send a poster and door hanger as selected overleaf. I enclose six tokens plus a 50p coin for P&P
- [ ] Please send me _____ pair(s) of Mr. Men/Little Miss fridge magnets, as selected above at £2.00 inc P&P

Fan's Name _____

Address _____

_____ **Postcode** _____

Date of Birth _____

Name of Parent/Guardian _____

Total amount enclosed £ _____

- [ ] **I enclose a cheque/postal order payable to Egmont Books Limited**
- [ ] **Please charge my MasterCard/Visa/Amex/Switch or Delta account** (delete as appropriate)

Card Number

Expiry date ___/___ **Signature** _____

Please allow 28 days for delivery. We reserve the right to change the terms of this offer at any time but we offer
a 14 day money back guarantee. This does not affect your statutory rights. Data Protection Act: If you do not wish
to receive other similar offers from us or companies we recommend, please tick this box [ ]. Offers apply to UK only.

MR.MEN   **LITTLE MISS**
Mr. Men and Little Miss™ & ©Mrs. Roger Hargreaves

CUT ALONG DOTTED LINE AND RETURN THIS WHOLE PAGE